THE GREAT CHEESE CONSPIRACY

THE GREAT CHEESE CONSPIRACY

JEAN VAN LEEUWEN

Marshall Cavendish Children

Marshall Cavendish Corporation, 99 White Plains Road, Tarrytown, NY 10591
www.marshallcavendish.us/kids

This book is a work of fiction. Names, characters, places, and incidents are
products of the author's imagination and are used fictitiously. Any resemblance
to actual events or locales or persons, living or dead, is entirely coincidental.

Marshall Cavendish *Classics*

Marshall Cavendish is bringing classic titles from children's literature back
into print for a new generation. We have selected titles that have withstood
the test of time, and we welcome any suggestions for future titles in this
program. To learn more, visit our website: www.marshallcavendish.us/kids.

Library of Congress Cataloging-in-Publication Data
Van Leeuwen, Jean.
The great cheese conspiracy / by Jean Van Leeuwen. — 1st Marshall Cavendish
classics ed.
p. cm.
Summary: Tired of gangster movies and a steady diet of candy wrappers, three
theater mice decide to rob a cheese shop.
ISBN 978-0-7614-5972-9 (hardcover) — ISBN 978-0-7614-6079-4 (ebook) [1.
Mice—Fiction. 2. Robbers and outlaws—Fiction. 3. Humorous stories.] I. Title.
PZ7.V275Gr 2011   [E]—dc22   2011002163

Book design by Becky Terhune

Printed in China (E)
10 9 8 7 6 5 4 3 2 1

Marshall Cavendish
Children

0 3143 3517

To Bruce, My Raymond

CONTENTS

CHAPTER ONE
I HAVE A BIG IDEA

It is on a rainy Saturday in September in the Bijou Theater in New York City that I have my big idea.

My gang and I are reclining on a plush red velvet seat in the first row of the balcony, watching the matinee showing of *Bank-busters*. All around is the comfortable smell of warm popcorn and wet umbrellas. When the soundtrack gets quiet, there's the cozy sound of people munching and crunching and whispering and sometimes snoring. It's an ordinary Saturday matinee.

I watch the cops slipping the handcuffs on Blackie McGraw and his two sidekicks as "The End" flashes on the screen.

"What a dumb way to lose the loot," I mutter in disgust. "I could have made the getaway easy."

Raymond the Rat sits up straight and takes off his spectacles. "There *did* seem to be a lack of efficient organization," he agrees.

Fats the Fuse is silent, so I know right away he's asleep. I apply a little of my torture twist to his tail and he mumbles, "Mmmphbut. Right, boss, right."

It is then, at that moment, that I have my big idea.

"Meeting in the Council Room right away," I order, and I walk away.

The Council Room is behind a potted palm at the back of the theater. My gang straggles in.

"What's the password?" I hiss at Fats.

He settles down with a candy-bar wrapper. "Sassafras tea?"

"That was last week."

"Constantinople," volunteers Raymond.

I nod at him approvingly, but then I notice that he is watching the previews of coming attractions out of the corner of his eye. I can see I'm going to have to show them again who's boss.

"Ahem!" I say in my toughest voice, snatching the candy wrapper from Fats and giving Raymond my hypnotic stare. Finally they give me the attention a leader deserves.

"I have something important to announce," I say. I pause to let that sink in, and then make my announcement. "I think we are ready for The Big Time."

"Big time?" repeats Fats. Sometimes it takes him a while to comprehend the significance of my remarks.

"The Big Time," I say firmly. "We are ready to pull a big job. No more of this

3

petty larceny—popcorn machines, candy bars—that's peanuts! We're going on to something bigger."

Raymond the Rat pulls on his whiskers as he always does when he is thinking. "You mean," he says finally, "we're going to rob a bank?"

"I *like* popcorn and candy bars," mumbles Fats.

No ambition, these two. No vision.

"No one has better training than this gang," I go on, trying to inspire them like a leader should. "We've watched hundreds of movie robberies and we know all the angles. We've seen all the mistakes and we—and *I*—know how to avoid making them. How can we fail?"

I am beginning to get through to Raymond the Rat. He is the scholarly type and thinks everything through very carefully. He nods his head slowly.

Fats the Fuse, on the other hand, asks his usual question, "Can we blast?" He only likes the parts in the movies where safes are blown up.

I don't even stoop to answer that one.

Raymond has a better question. "What kind of job do you have in mind?"

"I'm not sure," I admit. Then I drop my bombshell. "But," I add, "it's going to be on the Outside."

There is a long silence.

"The Outside," echoes Fats softly. He says it like he was speaking of candy bars.

Then Raymond speaks up. "You can't do it," he says. "No mouse who has gone outside this theater has ever returned alive." He shakes his head firmly. "No, Marvin, it's much too dangerous."

"Nonsense!" I snap. "And don't call me Marvin."

"Merciless Marvin the Magnificent," mutters Raymond the Rat grudgingly.

"That's better," I say. I draw myself up to my full height. "Boys, my mind is made up," I tell them. "I'm going Outside to find us a job worthy of our talents."

CHAPTER TWO
I GO OUTSIDE

I don't wait for them to think about it any more, or me either. The large proportions of my idea stagger even me. I go right into action.

Faster than a speeding bullet, I head down the aisle toward the side exit, staying under cover to escape detection. I slip easily between feet and umbrellas and packages, and once in a while an empty shoe. Another time I might have stopped to rearrange all this, but today I am all business. A true professional.

A moment later I am lurking under a seat across from the little red sign that reads EXIT, waiting for someone to go out. But no one is budging at the moment. The movie has them glued to their seats. I pace the floor, eager to get on with my adventure.

My eye falls on a shopping bag resting temptingly on its side beneath the next seat. I can't resist such an easy target and slip inside for a quick snack.

I sink my teeth eagerly into something soft, something rather dry, something that sticks to the roof of my mouth. I spit it out. It's a ball of knitting yarn. I've stumbled into a knitting bag.

I know right away I'm wasting my time. I start to take my leave when a strange thing happens. The bag tips, throwing me to the bottom where I land sharply on a couple of knitting needles. As I start to pick myself up, the bag begins to move.

"Excuse me, please," says a voice, an old lady's voice. And then the bag is traveling up the aisle.

Bounce, bounce, bounce. Each bounce lands me on the knitting needles. I grit my teeth and bear the pain. I'm tough. Jounce, jounce, jounce. I land on the ball of yarn and it wraps itself around me.

Then suddenly I hear a door close and feel the coldest air ever. Colder even than air conditioning. And I smile. I made it. I'm on the Outside.

I try to climb to the top of the bag to make my escape, but I'm hopelessly tangled in the knitting yarn. Then I hear the voice again. "Taxi!" it says.

I am desperate. If I am kidnapped by an old lady in a taxi, I may never find my way home again. I may never lead my gang to glory. I may never pull off the job of the century. I do the only thing I can think of. I take a great big bite out of that bag.

It's not as tasty as salted-peanut bags, but I force it down. Another mouthful and the hole is big enough to slip through. I land with a splash in a large puddle of water. It's not a very dignified beginning, but considering the narrowness of my escape I don't mind. I'm on the Outside.

I pick myself up and look around. I've seen it all in movies, of course, but this is the real thing. It looks the same—buildings reaching for the dark sky, flashing lights, blaring horns, and everything in a hurry. But it feels different. It feels wide and empty and full of promises. I almost forget what I'm here for, I'm so happy, and I breathe deep.

Then a car pulls up with a splash, and I know this isn't the time for dreams. I'm still standing in the gutter.

So I get on with my mission. Keeping in the shadows of the buildings so I won't be noticed, I case the street. First I check the stores near the theater. Next door is a flower shop. Not big enough. Then a dress store. I'm not interested. A bank. True, I know a lot about bank jobs, but what would we do with all that money? It has a dry taste.

And then I see it. Or rather, first I smell it.

Sharp, tangy, pungent, flavorful, appetizing, delectable *CHEESE*! I follow my nose blindly, knowing it is too good to be true. But there it is—a little shop full of nothing but cheese. There is even a sign, which I decipher easily after my long study of movie subtitles. It reads: THE CHEESE BARREL.

I stand on my tiptoes to peer through the glass door. As far as my eyes can see, there is nothing but cheese—boxes of it, barrels of it, hunks and slabs and jars and crocks of it. Here, under one roof, are all the cheeses of my dreams. To be on the

11

safe side, I pinch myself to make sure I'm awake. I am.

I pull myself together. There is no time to waste in drooling. This is The Big Time, the job I was meant to pull off. Mentally I run through the Rules of Procedure I've taught my gang, trying to recall Step Number One. Then it comes to me. Step Number One is: "Case the joint."

Keeping close to the wall, I make a full circle of the shop. I take note of the number of entrances and exits—two. I size up the construction of the building—red brick, run-down but solid. I memorize the store hours printed in fading gold letters on the front window: OPEN 9 A.M. TO 5:30 P.M. I check the alley filled with garbage cans that runs behind the shop. All this will be important later on. Then I creep back to the front door for further study of the loot.

The shop is closed and dark except for a single lightbulb that dangles from the ceiling over the cash register. By its dim light I can make out the shadowy figure of a man bent over the counter, writing in a large book. My heart beats faster. This is he. This is the Enemy.

For a long time I watch him, sizing him up, probing for weaknesses. He is big and mean-looking, with a round red face and a drooping mustache. Like the King of the Underworld in the movies. But his hair is white, and he wears spectacles that keep slipping down to the end of his nose. And he's even fatter than Fats. I can tell he will be no match for my gang. We can outrun him, and outsmart him, too.

At last he closes the book and reaches for his coat, and I know it's time to be on the move. I take the back-alley route back to the theater, keeping a sharp eye out for cats on the prowl. I wait beside an EXIT ONLY door, and after a while someone comes out and I go in.

CHAPTER THREE

I DEVISE A PLAN

Raymond the Rat and Fats the Fuse are in the Council Room when I arrive, and at first they don't see me.

Raymond is anxiously studying the front page of the New York *Globe*. "'Car Out of Control Hits Telephone Pole at 44th and Broadway,'" he reads. "'Driver and Two Spectators Injured.'" He shakes his head sadly. "Oh, Marvin, I knew we shouldn't have let you go. Will we ever see you again?"

Fats munches mournfully on the hard kernels of popcorn that people always leave in the bottom of the box. I think I see a tear in his eye. "I'll never forget how kind he was the time I got my tail caught in the popcorn machine," he says, sniffling a little. "It was such a heroic rescue."

This is more than I can take.

"I just did it so you wouldn't be captured and squeal on us," I say, stepping out from behind the potted palm.

Fats is so startled he forgets to munch, and Raymond's spectacles fall right off his nose. They look at me like they're seeing a ghost.

"An interesting trip," I say, as if I'd gone Outside every day of my life. "Rather fruitful, I think. I've found a job for us—if the gang is interested."

They are all questions then, and I tell them everything that happened— everything except my emergency landing in the puddle. That part doesn't sound dignified for a leader. As soon as Fats hears the word "cheese" he is all ears, and Raymond begins to take notes as I describe the layout of the shop.

"The joint is a cinch to knock over," I finish, borrowing a line from an old Humphrey Bogart movie I've seen a few times. "We can outsmart that old man with one hand tied behind our backs. Well, how about it? Do we pull off the job?"

Fats is so excited he can't answer. He's staring into space and humming a little song about "cheese, cheese, beautiful cheese." Then he gets up and does a ridiculous little dance.

"You look like a bowl of Jell-O," I tell him. "Sit down," and he does. "We are agreed then that we have at last found a job worthy of our talents?"

"The last piece of cheese I had was Muenster," says Fats dreamily. "Not as tangy as Cheddar but—"

"That was the last cheese you'll ever have," I interrupt, "unless we have a Plan. This job requires a Master Plan."

"A Plan, yes, a Plan," says Fats, beginning to snap out of it. "I know!" he shouts. "We'll blast!"

I scowl at him. "That's a terrible idea. What I had in mind was a stickup."

"Hooray!" cries Fats. He jumps up and goes into his cheese dance again.

Raymond the Rat has been pulling thoughtfully on his whiskers. This is usually a sign that he is going to say something, and I wait. "Hmmmm," he begins slowly, bending one whisker into a curl. "It seems to me that there are two factors to be considered. First of all, there is our size."

"What's wrong with our size?" asks Fats in a hurt tone, looking down at his ample stomach.

But Raymond pays no attention. "It is a disadvantage for a frontal attack,"

17

he goes on, "for transporting artillery or explosives, or seizing our objective by means of violence." Raymond is a military expert, having studied a lot of war movies. "Still, perhaps our size can be used to our advantage."

He thinks about this for a few minutes, polishing his spectacles thoughtfully. "Secondly, we must consider our objective. Do we want to make a single raid on the cheese shop, making off with as much cheese as we can carry?"

"Hooray!" cheers Fats.

"Or do we prefer infiltration?"

"What's infiltration?" asks Fats.

I give him a withering glance. "Silly question," I sneer. "Uh . . . You tell him, Raymond."

"Infiltration," explains Raymond, "is the act of penetrating the Enemy lines at a weak or unguarded point."

"Oh," says Fats.

"Once we penetrate the Enemy's defense and establish a way of entering the shop at will, we can strike any time our cheese supply runs low. That's the beauty of infiltration," finishes Raymond. "No storage problem."

He looks at me questioningly.

I consider a moment. "Raymond, old boy," I say, "I think you have something. We'll infilter!"

Raymond looks pleased. "Our size will be an asset for infiltration," he says. "We'll be almost invisible to the human eye, and we can slip through cracks and crannies where no other criminals would fit. Now—" He stands up like a schoolteacher in front of a class. "First, we must establish access to the shop. When you cased the area, Marvin, what weaknesses did you find in the Enemy lines?"

I scratch my ear, trying to remember. "There was a door in front and a door in back," I say positively.

"Mmmmm," says Raymond. "With perhaps a large crack underneath, or a mail slot our size?"

I consider for a moment. "No," I say.

"How about windows ajar or chinks in the wall?"

I shake my head. "The construction seemed solid."

Raymond assumes a thinking position again, pacing up and down and curling his whiskers. Fats and I are very quiet. "It's possible," he mumbles, "but then again . . ." He paces some more. Finally he says, almost to himself, "Yes, it just might work."

He eyes Fats with his schoolteacher look. "Fats," he says, "when is a door a weak or unguarded point?"

Fats gives this a few minutes' thought. "When it is open?" he guesses finally.

"Exactly," agrees Raymond. "It is my conclusion that we should infiltrate the store through the door, when it is open, during the day."

"In broad daylight?" I ask, shocked. This is unheard of. In the movies, the job is pulled off in the dark of the night when there is no moon.

"This is where our size will be an asset," Raymond explains. "The customers will be busy looking at cheese. The Enemy will be busy looking at customers. No one will notice us. We can quietly help ourselves to as much cheese as we can carry and silently slip away."

"Hooray!" shouts Fats, and I grab his tail to prevent another performance of the cheese dance.

Raymond looks at me expectantly. I frown, thinking it over. The plan is simple—too simple. In the movies, there are always ten different operations going on at once, and split-second timing, and alternate plans in case of emergency. Still, it has a certain daring that I like.

"But what if something goes wrong?" I ask. "What if we *are* noticed?"

"Hmmmm," says Raymond, pulling at a whisker. "Perhaps we should travel in disguise."

This is better. Disguises are always a big success in the movies. It's a good thing the movie on now is a musical, because the meeting gets very loud as we discuss our disguises. Raymond is in favor of something simple like caps pulled down over our eyes, while Fats thinks we should stand on each other's shoulders and pose as a customer.

But they both have to admit that my idea is brilliant. I get it when Fats withdraws from the discussion and prepares to take a nap in the abandoned popcorn box.

"That's it!" I exclaim, and Fats opens one eye reluctantly. "We'll go as a popcorn box. No one will notice an old box that happens to blow into the store. It's a perfect disguise."

Raymond looks at me with admiration. "It might work, Marvin," he says. "It just might."

"Might shmight!" I say firmly. "It can't fail."

CHAPTER FOUR

I LEAD AN EXPEDITION

"Get ready!" I whisper. "Someone's coming."

Disguised as a popcorn box, we are waiting by the exit door for someone to go out.

"It's hot in here," complains Fats the Fuse.

"Sssssh!" I give him a sharp elbow, and peer out through the o in CORN, where Raymond the Rat has made an inconspicuous peephole. A black trouser leg has stopped next to us and I hold my breath, but it moves on up the aisle.

"My mother used to say you can travel east and travel west but home is always best," says Raymond, at his peephole in the O in POP. I give him my other elbow in his ear. The box is not as roomy as I had hoped, and it has taken hours of practice to get my gang to walk in step. Still, I have confidence.

Just then, there is a brown alligator shoe in front of my eyes, a loud click, and a gust of wind that almost blows us back across the aisle.

"Now!" I say, and we just make it through the door before it slams.

"Well done," I whisper. And then Fats trips over his own tail and our progress stops.

We get in step again and head for the shop. The wind is strong, and we don't have to pretend that we are blown into the store. We are blown right past it.

"Stop!" I shout, but a gust of wind lifts us up and suddenly we're flying.

"Help!" cries Fats, holding on for dear life. Raymond has his eyes shut tight. But I peer out the o and laugh. Who ever thought that I, Merciless Marvin, would be flying?

Our flight ends all too soon. The popcorn box does a double somersault, bounces off a mailbox, and makes a crash-landing on the sidewalk in front of the cheese shop. Fats and Raymond rub their bumped noses.

"Getting there is half the fun," I tell them cheerfully. Then, before they can get cold feet, I order, "On with the mission."

Slowly, silently, the popcorn box glides across the sidewalk, up over the door sill, and onto the sawdusty floor of the cheese shop. There we stop short, intoxicated by the smell that greets our nostrils.

Edam and Provolone and Wisconsin Cheddar and Gouda and Gruyère and Parmesan and Liederkranz and Muenster and Ricotta and Roquefort and Coon

Cheddar and Limburger and Swiss and Port Salut and Camembert and Gorgonzola and Cracker Barrel Cheddar all wrapped up in one beautiful aroma. And all within our grasp.

"Let me look," says Fats, elbowing me aside so he can gaze out my o. "I wouldn't have believed it," he sighs reverently.

The two of us take turns looking until Raymond the Rat reminds us what we're here for.

"First," he says in a businesslike tone, "we must make a survey of the situation." He peers out his o for a long time, while Fats and I slowly rotate the box so he can get the picture from all angles.

At last he turns to me with a worried look. "Marvin," he announces, "we can't do it. It's too dangerous."

"What?" I can't believe my ears.

"We are surrounded by feet. At any moment we may be stepped on and

27

trampled to death. We will have to retreat. I'm afraid," he adds apologetically, "that I underestimated the volume of customers."

Fats the Fuse begins to tremble.

I ask myself how I could have allowed mice of so little courage to join my gang. Putting my eye to the o, I survey the situation for myself.

I have to admit that Raymond has a point. Feet of all sizes and shapes surround us—thick-soled oxfords to flatten us like pancakes, sharp-pointed heels to fill us full of holes. But we've come too far and the stakes are too high to back out now.

"When the going gets tough, the tough get going," I tell them, inspiring them like a leader should. Then I apply just a suggestion of the torture twist to Fats's tail.

"Right, boss, right," he says quickly.

I take another look out the o. "If we stick close to the wall we'll be safe," I decide. "We'll head for the barrel of Cheddar."

Under my hypnotic stare, Fats and Raymond meekly take their places and once again the popcorn box starts to move. I have one anxious moment, when a dagger-sharp heel misses us by a whisker. "Steer left," I hiss, and we circle around a pair of riding boots, dodge two dirty white sneakers, and slip safely behind the barrel of Cheddar.

I wait a moment for my heart to resume its natural beat.

Then I notice that Fats has gone into some kind of trance, his eyes closed, his whiskers twitching. And suddenly I remember. Wisconsin Cheddar is his very favorite.

"Fats," I tell him, "you are going to have the honor of making the first raid."

He blinks.

"You'll go after some Cheddar. Raymond will keep watch at the o. I will supervise."

He begins to tremble again.

"Wisconsin Cheddar," I remind him. "Your absolute favorite."

He stops trembling and makes a dash for the end of the box. I am forced to sit on him. "Wait till the coast is clear."

Raymond is staring out the o. "Brown Oxfords coming this way," he reports. A minute later, "She's dropped a hunk of Cheddar. Get ready for action."

Fats's whiskers twitch. I stand ready to open the end of the box.

"Uh-oh," says Raymond suddenly, "we're in trouble. Hang on."

And then the box is lifted into the air, and Fats and I are thrown on top of Raymond. In a moment we feel the cold air of the Outside again.

"They just don't sweep these stores clean," complains Brown Oxfords, and then we are falling.

"Good-bye forever," sobs Fats.

But we land on something soft, all tangled up in a pile and full of surprise. The end of the box has come open, and I crawl

out and look around. The place where we
have landed is rather embarrassing.

"Where are we?" asks Fats.

I lead them out and show them the
sign. It reads: HELP KEEP NEW YORK CLEAN.
THROW TRASH HERE.

CHAPTER FIVE

I VOLUNTEER FOR A DANGEROUS MISSION

The next day we meet again in the Council Room. Gloom is written on the faces of my gang. Fats is consoling himself with a half-eaten Nestlé's Crunch, while Raymond glumly studies the financial pages of yesterday's New York *Globe*. It is obvious I am going to have to give them a pep talk.

"Ahem," I begin. "It is true that we have had a slight setback in our Master Plan. But are we going to let that stop us from pulling off the crime of the century?

Are we going to stand by while a whole store full of cheese goes uneaten?"

"No!" shouts Fats.

"Of course not," I agree. "I will lead us on to victory. Remember, if at first you don't succeed, try, try again."

"Hooray!" cheers Fats.

Raymond looks up from his newspaper. "Perhaps," he suggests, "we should try a different approach. Infiltrating in broad daylight is too dangerous."

"Exactly," I agree. "From now on, we'll infiltrate in the dark of night. But then," I reason, "the door will be locked."

"Yes," says Raymond. He strokes his whiskers slowly. "I think, however, I may have the answer to that problem. I think there is a key."

Fats stops in mid-munch to stare at him. "A key?" he repeats.

"Of course," I snap. "There was bound to be a key. But where?"

Raymond takes his pencil from behind his ear and starts to scribble on a corner of the *Globe*. When he is finished, he has drawn a floor plan of the cheese shop. He points to an X in one corner.

"This represents our position when we entered the shop," he explains. "In surveying the situation from this point, something shiny caught my eye." He moves his pencil point across the paper. "It was hanging here, on the wall above the cash register. It seems possible that it could be a key to the front door."

"Of course it is," I break in. "The job is a cinch. All we have to do is slip into the shop at closing time, grab the key, and slip out when the shop opens in the morning. Then we'll be able to help ourselves to cheese anytime we want." I see now that we have a foolproof plan.

"All we need now," I tell my gang, "is a volunteer for this dangerous mission."

I wait for a volunteer to step forward.

"It's not really *so* dangerous," I say encouragingly, but Raymond the Rat is avoiding my eye. I look at Fats, who is nibbling listlessly on his candy bar. "I'm so tired of Nestlé's Crunch," he complains.

"I'd do it myself," I go on, "but—"

"Why don't you?" asks Fats. "As our leader and all."

I consider this idea. I know it is traditional for a leader to stay in the hideout and direct operations. On the other hand, isn't it up to me to inspire my gang, to set an example of courage and daring? Perhaps I may even be awarded a medal for heroism.

"I'll do it!" I say, and Fats stands up and cheers.

Raymond the Rat immediately starts to make plans. "You'll need certain equipment," he reflects, putting on his spectacles. He studies the diagram of the cheese shop and draws a few more arrows. At last he says, "Yes, I believe we have the equipment on hand," and disappears in the direction of his hole.

I follow. If there is one thing Raymond the Rat can be counted on for, it is equipment. He saves things. Stashed away in his hole is the world's largest movie-theater lost-and-found department. Most of it isn't even good to eat, but Raymond doesn't care. He thinks it will all come in handy someday.

Fats and I can hardly fit inside, the hole is so crowded. "Don't you ever throw anything away?" I complain, relaxing in the scuffed brown shoe that serves Raymond for a bed.

Raymond shakes his head sorrowfully. "I can't."

If ever a mousehole needed a housecleaning, it's this one. Leaning piles of newspapers tower almost to the ceiling. There are packages of Kleenex, a flashlight that doesn't work, seven unmatched mittens, a ball of tinfoil from chewing gum packs, a pocket dictionary, several mousetraps, a doll with one leg, a fleet of toy racing cars, a lady's hat made out of feathers, three lipsticks, a diamond ring, and a lot of plastic favors from Cracker Jack boxes. In one corner, which Raymond calls his workshop, are springs and screws and safety pins and wire and thread and a lot of pieces of things. And way in back are our emergency rations—boxes of tea and shredded wheat and cough drops for days when both the popcorn and candy machines are out of order.

Raymond shuffles through all this junk, raising such a cloud of dust that Fats goes into a sneezing fit. But when he finally comes out from behind a stack of library books, he's got all the equipment.

"First of all," he says, brushing a cobweb off the tip of his nose, "a simple disguise." He hands me a tan raincoat and felt hat that once belonged to the doll with one leg.

I slip into the coat, pull the hat down low on my head, and go to look in the cracked mirror from a lady's compact that stands next to Raymond's bed. I must admit I look quite dashing, rather like a foreign agent.

"No one will ever recognize you, Marvin," says Fats approvingly.

The next piece of equipment is a coil of stout string. "For scaling walls," explains Raymond, "and lassoing the key." I sling it rakishly over my shoulder.

Finally, Raymond presents me with a tiny envelope with one word printed on it: "Pepper."

"What's that for?" asks Fats.

"Questions, questions," I say impatiently. "Tell him, Raymond."

"That's our secret weapon," explains Raymond with a touch of pride. "In an emergency, you throw it in the Enemy's face, and while he is sneezing you make your escape."

"Of course." I congratulate myself on discovering Raymond and training him for my gang. A leader needs a right-hand man he can trust.

When all my equipment is strapped in place and I'm ready to go, Fats slips me something in a little package.

"What's that?" I ask.

"A piece of Nestlé's Crunch," he says. "To keep your strength up."

I stash it away under my hat. Then Raymond the Rat says, "It's time," and I'm off to become a Hero.

CHAPTER SIX

I AM TRAPPED

It is closing time and I lurk in the shadows, waiting for the Enemy to go home. The sign says the shop closes at five-thirty, but it is long after that now. I know, because the shadows are growing longer and I am hungry and my equipment is beginning to feel heavy.

I risk a look inside. The Enemy is still there all right. He is sitting at the counter, his spectacles low on his nose, writing in his ledger.

Stepping back into the shadows, I take off my hat and have a quick nibble of

Nestlé's Crunch for extra energy. Then I hear a noise inside. He is coming toward the door.

Bravely I hold my ground. The Enemy opens the door, then turns to snap out the light. This is my chance and I do not hesitate. I slip between his legs, the door slams, and I am safe inside.

So far my attack has been flawless. Staying in the shadows near the door, I survey the situation. Everything is quiet. I am alone with the cheese, and the temptation to help myself to a few samples almost makes me forget my mission. But I am strong. My mission comes first.

The shop is dark except for a dim light in back, but that is enough to see what I'm looking for. Hanging on a nail above the cash register, just where Raymond remembered it, is a key.

Now I am glad I thought to bring all my equipment. I creep over to the counter and uncoil my rope. I measure the distance in my mind's eye. It will be a tricky shot, but I think I can do it. I haven't sat through hundreds of Westerns for nothing.

Expertly I make a loop in the end of my rope. I swing it around my head a few times like they do in the movies, then let it fly.

It's a professional throw, but it falls a little short. I gather up my rope and try again. And then again. It's not quite the same as roping cattle. But on my fifth throw, fortune smiles. The loop nudges the key off its nail, and it drops with a *plunk* on the counter.

Now all I have to do is retrieve the key. I gather in my rope and make a larger loop in the end. Skillfully, I lasso the cash register. Then, hand over hand, I scale the counter. Luckily I've seen plenty of mountain-climbing movies, too.

At the top there is the key waiting for me, lying next to an old moth-eaten fur piece someone has left behind. I climb over the fur piece and slip the key under my arm. Now I'm ready to make my getaway. The mission has gone like clockwork, and I wonder how we could ever have thought it was dangerous. It's easier than stealing gumdrops from a candy machine.

As I climb back over the fur piece, something peculiar happens. The fur piece twitches. It moves. It stretches. I take a closer look at it, and slowly the terrible truth dawns on me. The old moth-eaten fur piece is in reality an old, moth-eaten, but very ferocious Cat.

There is no time to think about this natural mistake, for the Cat is hissing with fury and once he wakes up will undoubtedly want to eat me. In desperation I remember my secret weapon. Just as the Cat's gigantic jaws open to swallow me up, I rip open the envelope and let him have it.

It works just like we planned. The Cat goes into a fit of sneezing, wheezing, sniffling, and coughing, and I have just enough time to scramble down my rope before he is after me.

Around barrels and behind boxes we go, his breath hot on my heels. I look desperately for a hiding place. Luckily he is old and stout, and I outrun him to a narrow crack between two barrels of Cheddar. His vicious claws splinter the wood as he tries to dislodge me, but I am out of reach. Finally he gives up and settles down a few inches away, to glare and wait.

I know I can't stay here forever, but for the moment I am safe, and we both settle down uneasily for a long night.

CHAPTER SEVEN

I OUTWIT
A FEROCIOUS BEAST

It is the longest night of my life. The Cat's great paw is less than two inches from my nose, and we both know I can't escape. He dozes, but I cannot. My thoughts are dark. They have to do with all those beautiful cheeses I will never eat, the medal I will never win, the glory that will never come to my gang now.

Finally I doze off for a minute and I dream that the Cat is sitting on a throne at the end of a long banquet table, in a room lit by hundreds of flickering candles. The Enemy places before him a gleaming silver dish. The Cat lifts the cover and there I am, all tied up with ribbons and an apple in my mouth.

I wake up screaming. Somehow my senses return after this, and I remember that no predicament is so hopeless that it cannot be turned into a victory. I think of all the times I've seen it done in the movies, when the hero is trapped in a safe with a bomb ticking away next to him and only thirty seconds to live. My problem is different, of course, but all I need to escape is courage and daring.

And slowly, as the new day dawns to illuminate every detail of the Cat's deadly claws, a Plan begins to take shape in my mind.

It seems likely that for some strange reason the Enemy is fond of this miserable Cat. When he comes to the shop in the morning, he will probably stop to pet the creature, or give him a saucer of milk. I will be prepared for this moment. If the Cat looks the other way for a second, I will be ready to make my escape. If, on the other hand, the Enemy comes to see what the Cat has trapped . . . I don't finish this thought. It is too much like my dream.

Just before nine o'clock, I hear a key turn in the front door. I am ready, my hat pulled low for courage, my knees shaking a little due to lack of sleep.

I hear the Enemy's voice.

"Good morning, Giovanni," it says.

The Cat rudely ignores the greeting.

After a few minutes the voice comes again. "Ready for breakfast?" it asks. There are sounds of milk being poured. But the Cat does not budge. Heavy footsteps slowly approach my hiding place, and my heart beats double-time.

"It is most strange," the Enemy mumbles to himself. "String and paper all over the floor. I am sure I swept last night. And this key, it should not be lying about. I must put it away in a safe place."

The footsteps come closer, then stop. "You thought last night you were a kitten again, eh, Giovanni?"

Suddenly, miraculously, he has picked up the Cat and is scolding him. This is my chance and I waste no time. While the Enemy scolds and the Cat mutters to himself, I dart from my hiding place to a safer one high on a shelf behind a package of Kimmel Kase from Holland.

The rest is easy. Before long, the door opens and customers begin to come in. As I mingle with the crowd, my disguise serves perfectly, and I make my escape.

CHAPTER EIGHT
I DEVISE A NEW PLAN

"Did you get the key?" ask Fats and Raymond in unison.

"It was a close call," I reply, removing my disguise. "I barely escaped with my life."

"You didn't get the key?" Fats has a one-track mind.

I try to impress on them that the important thing is that their leader has returned. "And it was only by a feat of great courage and daring," I tell them, "that I managed to escape capture and—yes—death at the hands of a ferocious beast."

Fats's eyes open wide. "A beast?"

"A beast," I repeat. "A Cat, employed by the Enemy to guard the cheese."

They both stare at me with new respect as I recite the harrowing story of my perilous night. When I am finished, Fats offers me a dirty jelly bean. "You must be tired," he says sympathetically.

Raymond the Rat has been taking notes. He studies them thoughtfully "Black Cat. Age: approximately 12 years. Weight: about 20 pounds. Disposition: mean. All teeth and claws operational." He strokes his whiskers. "Marvin, there is only one possible course of action. This Cat must be eliminated."

"Exactly what I was going to suggest," I say quickly.

Fats perks up. "Can we blast him?" he asks.

Raymond shakes his head. "Explosives are too noisy. We must be quiet and discreet."

He puts on his thinking pose, and Fats and I do likewise. There is silence while we all consider the problem. I am just planning how we could slip a dose of knockout drops in his milk, like they did in *One Night in Casablanca,* when Raymond says, "I think I've got it."

He produces a piece of paper on which he has drawn the strangest-looking gadget I have ever seen. It's all ropes and wheels and arrows pointing in every direction. "What's that?" asks Fats.

"Elementary, my dear Fats," I answer. "Tell him, Raymond."

"That," says Raymond with a touch of pride, "may be the most significant invention of my career. It's a cat trap."

Again, I congratulate myself on single-handedly molding Raymond, an ordinary theater mouse, into a master criminal.

The trap, explains Raymond, is designed on the classic principle of the mousetrap.

We are familiar with mousetraps, having had our last ration of cheese from one in the projection room several weeks ago. But our trap will be made from one of the garbage cans that are piled in the alley behind the shop.

I think the idea through carefully. It sounds foolproof. There is just one small detail that bothers me.

"Cats don't like cheese," I remind Raymond. "What will we use for bait?"

Raymond gnaws on the end of his pencil thoughtfully.

"What I was thinking of using," he says finally, "was you."

CHAPTER NINE

I BAIT A TRAP

So again I am a volunteer. After this mission I am confident of a medal. Or perhaps I would prefer an extra cut of the loot—I haven't decided yet.

As we have worked out the Plan, my part is easy.

It is the Cat's habit to take a late afternoon stroll in the alley behind the shop, to make inspection, look for tidbits for an afternoon snack, and sharpen his terrible claws for his next victim. Near the back door is a pile of old cheese cartons, cheese barrels, and cheese boxes. And resting on top of the pile is an upside-down green plastic garbage can. This we have made into our cat trap.

Raymond has spent hours in his workshop, devising a system of levers and weights, ropes, and pulleys. According to the Plan, I will be hiding behind a certain cheese carton as the Cat makes his daily rounds. I will attract his attention to the bait. Then, just as he leaps to devour me, I will step lightly aside and give my gang the signal. The garbage can will fall, and we'll have our Cat caught neatly in the trap.

Everything is in readiness. Raymond has tested his ropes, and I have practiced stepping lightly aside until I can do it in my sleep. The movie goes on, and I know it's time to move.

"Assume battle stations," I command, and we slip quietly out of the theater.

Raymond and Fats take their positions behind a barrel of Imported Swiss, and

I give them their final instructions. "Remember," I tell them, "when I say 'when,' let the garbage can fall."

"Aye, aye," says Fats with a little salute.

"Check," says Raymond.

I proceed to my battle station, in the shadows of a packing box that once contained Provolone from Italy. It adds an appetizing aroma to the air, but I try not to think about it. I am listening carefully for the approach of the Cat. Minutes go by and the shadows in the alley start to lengthen. And then I hear it, the slashing, ripping, splintering sound that can only be the Cat sharpening his claws to a fine point on a cheese barrel.

I give the warning signal, the low hoot of an owl that they always use in the movies. Raymond hoots back, and I peer cautiously from my hiding place.

There he is, meandering slowly down the alley, pausing frequently for a sniff at an appetizing garbage can. Little does he know he is about to be captured.

As he reaches the box where I am lurking, he stops to give the toenails on his right front paw a manicure.

Swiftly I go into action.

"Pssst!" I hiss.

He goes on with his manicure.

"Pssssssst, Cat!" I say, a little louder. "Come and get me!"

He doesn't even look up.

We hadn't counted on this problem, and I think fast.

"Ahem!" I shout, stepping out of the shadows.

He sees me then and gathers himself for the fatal lunge. But before he can spring, there is a terrible noise and everything turns black. For a second, I am conscious of the overpowering odor of garbage, and then I know no more.

CHAPTER TEN
I DEVISE
A FOOLPROOF PLAN

When I come to, I am in the Council Room. Fats and Raymond are hovering anxiously over me. The moment my eyes flutter open, Fats shoves a salted peanut in my face.

I push it away. "What happened?" I ask. "How did I get here?"

"Oh dear," sighs Fats. "He has amnesia. He doesn't remember a thing." Fats has always liked amnesia movies.

Raymond the Rat feels my pulse and shakes his head sadly. "Can't you even remember your name?" he asks. "Or some little incident of the past?"

"Of course I remember my name," I snap indignantly, "and I remember everything in my past except what hit me."

Raymond takes off his spectacles. "Thank goodness for that," he says with relief. Fats relaxes and eats my salted peanut.

"It was the garbage can that hit you," explains Raymond. "We heard your signal and pulled the release lever, and then we saw the Cat walk away."

"So Raymond used his ropes and we rescued you and brought you here," finishes Fats.

"Unfortunately, there was a little garbage stuck to the bottom of the can," Raymond adds apologetically. "When the trap was sprung, it fell on your head."

I sit up and remove a lettuce leaf from my shoulder and an orange peel from behind my ear. After a few minutes the room stops going around and I can think clearly about the situation. It is obvious that my gang has failed me again. "I *didn't* give the signal," I tell them, fixing Fats with my evil stare.

"We heard you say 'when,'" insists Fats, but he cannot meet my eye.

"What I said was 'ahem'," I inform him coldly. "I was trying to draw the Cat's attention to the bait."

Fats looks ashamed, Raymond looks thoughtful, and I look disgusted. It is discouraging for a leader to have such an incompetent gang. I am just wondering how long it would take to train a new one, when Raymond speaks up.

"The question is," he says, "why didn't the Cat fall for the trap?"

Neither Fats nor I can answer that question.

"Technically, it was foolproof," Raymond mutters to himself. "And the bait was tempting. Yet he didn't fall for it. Why?"

He takes off his spectacles and puts them on again, twirls his whiskers into curls, and goes through all the other routines that show he's deep in thought. After his twelfth trip up and down the Council Room, he suddenly stops in front of me.

"Marvin, I think I've got it. There *is* a logical explanation. The Cat must be hard of hearing."

I can't believe my ears.

"Isn't it true that the Cat did not notice you when you tried to get his attention— not until you shouted at him?"

I nod.

"And isn't it true that when you infiltrated the shop he didn't notice you until you stepped on him?"

I begin to feel a little more cheerful.

"The logical conclusion then is that the Cat is hard of hearing," concludes

Raymond triumphantly. "This condition is not uncommon in cats of advancing years," he adds in his schoolteacher's voice. "Under the circumstances, I believe we have overestimated his nuisance value. He needn't be eliminated after all."

"Hooray!" cheers Fats.

I think it over. I consider the matter carefully. Then I make my decision. "We will proceed despite him," I announce. "Quietly."

"We need a new plan for gaining entrance to the shop," says Raymond. "A bold, revolutionary plan."

"We could blast," Fats pipes up hopefully, but Raymond silences him.

"A bold, revolutionary, *quiet* plan," he says.

Fats has finished off a batch of popcorn kernels, and begins to gnaw on the box. "If we don't get another idea soon," he complains, "we may starve. I'm so hungry I could eat the door."

I look at him scornfully. It would take a year of broken popcorn machines before he'd begin to lose weight.

But Raymond is staring at Fats with a strange glint in his eye.

"Do I have crumbs on my whiskers?" Fats asks nervously.

"Repeat what you just said," says Raymond.

"Do I have crumbs on my whiskers?" Fats repeats.

"No," says Raymond. "About the door."

"I said I'm so hungry I could eat the door." Fats looks at Raymond and adds hastily, "But I didn't really mean it. It was just a manner of speaking."

"Why not?" asks Raymond. "You eat popcorn boxes, and after all, paper is a form of wood. A wooden door should be just as easy."

Fats looks alarmed, and Raymond says reassuringly, "Oh, you wouldn't have to eat the whole door. Just a big enough space under it for us to slip through. Then we could come and go as we please. We would never be without cheese."

I can see that this time we have come up with the perfect plan. Considered from all angles, it's foolproof. The only problem that remains is Fats, who is saying, "I won't do it! I won't do it!"

I handle him with my usual skill.

"It's dry and tasteless," he is saying, "and I'll get splinters in my tongue."

"Fats," I say softly, "think of cheese. Think of Provolone, think of Limburger, think of Bel Paese, think of Edam, think of Roquefort, think of Romano, think of *Wisconsin Cheddar*!"

"I'll do it," says Fats.

CHAPTER ELEVEN

I COMMIT THE CRIME
OF THE CENTURY

He is true to his word. For the next few nights we all work diligently, Fats gnawing on the wood at the lower edge of the back door, Raymond and I disposing of the telltale chips like they do in the prison escape movies. Most important, I serve as an inspiration to Fats when his teeth are tired and his spirits sag. Then I talk to him about the golden glory that is Wisconsin Cheddar, the exciting experience that is Camembert, and all the other delicacies that wait for us just a splinter away. And finally, one night, our tunnel is finished.

It is large enough for Fats to squeeze through if he holds his breath, yet small enough to be just a crack under the door to the human eye. As I survey our handiwork, I know beyond a shadow of a doubt that we are about to commit the crime of the century.

The next evening, I call my gang together in the Council Room for their final instructions.

"Remember," I tell them, "silence is golden."

Raymond nods solemnly.

"He who fights and runs away will live to fight another day."

Fats nods eagerly.

"And two birds in the hand are worth one in the bushes."

Fats looks a little confused at this, so I add, "Strike while the cheese is hot!"

"Hooray!" He jumps up and does a few steps of the cheese dance.

"Just a minute," says Raymond, and he scurries away to his hole. When he comes back, he is carrying three small sacks. "I stitched them together this morning," he explains with a touch of pride, "out of handkerchiefs." I notice that mine has a large *M* embroidered on the corner. "If we take just as much cheese as will fit in these sacks," he goes on, "the Enemy will never miss it."

"Good thinking," I congratulate him, and Raymond blushes. "Now let's get moving."

I lead the way, expertly weaving between chair legs and people feet to the exit door. Gray trouser legs go out and so do we.

"So far so good," I whisper. "Lie low while I see if the coast is clear."

They get lost in the shadows and I drift up the alley to the street. The alley is quiet—no cats or night watchmen on patrol, nothing but the sound of dead leaves scurrying along with the wind. But the city is wide awake. Signs blink, horns honk, the sidewalk teems with people all dressed up and going somewhere. Their minds are on where they're going, though, and they don't see me as I mingle with the throng and drift along to the cheese shop.

I give it a quick once-over. Everything seems quiet. The shop is dark. No cops are in sight.

I slink back to the alley.

"Psst," I hiss into the darkness. "The coast is clear."

Two shadows appear beside me. Single file we take the back-alley route to the door where our tunnel waits. We pause beside it for a last look around. Then one by one— me first, then Raymond, then Fats—we slip under the door.

Inside the shop everything is dark and quiet. An occasional soft snore comes from the top of the counter, where the Cat slumbers peacefully, his tail resting lightly on the cash register. Single file we steal across the floor below him.

And there before us is the loot, ripe for the taking. Feta cheese from Greece, Mascarpone from Italy, Emmenthaler from Switzerland, Crema Danica from Denmark, Kimmel Kase from Holland, Camembert from France, Cheshire cheese from England. Beautiful, flavorful, delectable cheese!

It is a moment of magnificent triumph. I am tempted to do a performance of the cheese dance myself, but I resist. We can't let success go to our heads.

I give Fats and Raymond the elbow. "Remember," I mutter into Fats's ear, "just fill the sack." He nods, and we spring into action.

Quickly we move from box to barrel to crock, taking a crumb of this, a morsel of that. I sample the Herkimer cheese from New York, tuck a little Gorgonzola into my sack, and make an extra hole that the Enemy will never notice in the Imported Swiss. Then as I stash away a crumb of Muenster with Caraway Seeds for a bedtime snack, something tells me it's time for our getaway.

I give the signal. Fats is busy on the top shelf, submerged in a pot of Port-wine Cheddar.

"Pssst," I whisper. "Let's blow."

Reluctantly he climbs out of the pot. Then it happens. Under the weight of Fats the pot tips. For a terrible moment it teeters on the edge of the shelf. And then it crashes to the floor.

Raymond and I freeze where we are, lost in the shadows. Not daring to breathe, we keep our eyes on the Cat. He stirs, he stretches, his claws gleam long and terrible in the dim light.

I close my eyes. I can't bear to watch him devour Fats. And then, as I wait for it all to be over, a soft snore comes again from the counter top.

I open my eyes. I breathe again. But just as I do, a giant shadow appears at the front door. "Don't move," I hiss at Fats. Raymond and I duck back behind a barrel and study that shadow. There is something familiar about it; it reminds me of a movie I have seen. And then I remember—it's the cops.

It's one cop anyway. He's peering inside and twirling a nightstick. He stands there for what seems like hours, and then he scratches his head and strolls away.

Again, I breathe easy. Raymond nudges me and points to the back door. I nod. "Let's blow," I whisper again.

Fats extracts himself from the cheese pot and we make for the door.

I slip under, Raymond follows, and we steal through the alleys like part of the night. We reach the exit door as someone leaves, and we are home free.

"Whew," I sigh, sinking down into the thick carpet of the Council Room floor. "That was a close one."

We rest for a few minutes, just breathing hard and mopping our brows, and then suddenly Raymond sits up straight. "Fats!" he says. "Where is Fats?"

CHAPTER TWELVE

I LEAD A HEROIC RESCUE

I look around. "He was right behind you," I say. "He should be here any minute." A minute goes by and Fats does not appear.

Raymond the Rat looks worried. Another minute passes and he begins to pace the floor. After the third minute, he says, "Marvin, we must face the truth. Fats, our dear friend, our loyal comrade, has been captured."

I nod sadly. "Arrested and sent to prison. Poor Fats."

I reach in my sack for a crumb of Muenster to keep my strength up.

Raymond keeps pacing. A tear is forming in his eye. "We must go to his rescue," he says.

"Sent up the river on a grand larceny charge," I mumble a bit sleepily. The carpet is soft and I am tired after our narrow escape.

"We must rescue Fats!" Raymond says, poking his nose in my face. "At once, before it's too late!"

"At once, before he squeals on us!" I jump up, wide awake and ready to lead again.

Outside in the alley, we look both ways. There are no cops in sight. Perhaps there is still time to rescue Fats.

Cautiously we creep back to the shop, and pause by our tunnel to listen. The night is quiet, too quiet.

"This may be a trap," I mutter to Raymond. But bravely I start to slip under the door.

As I do so, I notice a nose sticking out of the crack. I would know that nose anywhere. It belongs to Fats.

"Fats," I whisper. "Are you there?"

The nose twitches and a weak voice replies, "Help."

"What happened?" I ask.

"I got stuck!" wails the voice.

I should have known this would happen, that Fats could not be trusted to follow orders. He has eaten too much cheese.

"Don't be afraid," calls Raymond. "We will rescue you."

"Turn around," I order. "Give us your tail."

We both grab his tail and start to pull. Fats lets out a loud squeak.

"Quiet!" I snap.

"You must try to be brave," says Raymond.

We try it again, but it's no use. Fats is wedged in that tunnel like Coon Cheddar in a crock.

Then I notice something I've never seen before. Running along the bottom of the door and into the crack is a thin wire. This must be what is interfering with Fats's progress. I point it out to Raymond the Rat.

"Don't—" he starts to say, but I am not afraid. I take hold of that wire and pull.

The world seems to come to an end. A clanging noise louder than any soundtrack rings in our ears. Whistles blow, tires screech, feet pound down the alley. Before we can move to make our getaway, we are surrounded.

Three cops close in, their guns drawn. A spotlight is beamed on the back door, and a voice growls through a megaphone, "All right, come through that door with your hands up."

We have no choice. Raymond and I step forward into the spotlight with our paws in the air.

CHAPTER THIRTEEN

I SNATCH VICTORY FROM THE JAWS OF DEFEAT

It is the most desperate moment of my career. For a few seconds the cops just stare at us. Then one of them, as big as a mountain with bright red hair, leans down and picks up Raymond and me by our tails. I have never been so humiliated. Another cop notices the plump tail protruding from the crack. He gives it a little tug and out pops Fats.

We dangle in the air while the cops look at each other. And then someone else pushes his way through the ring of cops. He is big and mean-looking, like the King of the Underworld, and he is wearing an overcoat over striped pajamas. My heart sinks slowly to my toes. It is the Enemy.

His face is red and his mustache is quivering. "What is going on here?" he demands.

Red Hair looks him over. "And who might you be, Mac?" he asks.

"I am Mr. Sammartino, and this shop, it belongs to me," sputters the Enemy. "Where are the thieves? I hear the alarm from across the street and I come to break them into little pieces!"

He is waving his arms and shouting by now, and I shiver suddenly in the night air.

Then Raymond and I are swooped up and held barely an inch from his nose.

"Here are your thieves," says Red Hair calmly.

The Enemy stops waving his arms and blinks at us. He reaches into his coat for a pair of spectacles and puts them on. He stares at us with icy steel-gray eyes. Finally he says in a much quieter voice, "These? These are the burglars?"

"That's them," replies Red Hair. A chuckle starts somewhere deep inside of him and spreads up to his face, and Raymond and I bob up and down. "Tough customers, eh? Me and the boys caught them red-handed. Want us to book them for attempted burglary?"

The Enemy shakes his head slowly, still looking like he can't believe his eyes.

The cops start shuffling around and holstering their guns.

"Well, we'll be on our way now," says Red Hair. "Want us to dispose of the criminals for you?"

The Enemy shakes his head again. "No," he says, and his voice is soft but sinister, "I take care of them."

He holds out his hat, and one by one the cops drop us into it. We hear heavy feet walking away and a motorcycle growl into action.

"Thank you for the assistance," calls the Enemy.

"Any time," answers a cop, and the motorcycle roars away down the alley.

Then the hat is moving, and we hear a key turn in the back door. We huddle together in the bottom of the hat. At last we are going to be a meal for that miserable Cat. Raymond the Rat is trying not to tremble, while Fats the Fuse sniffles loudly.

"Good-bye forever," he sobs.

And then it is all over. The hat tips and we are falling—down, down, down into the dark jaws of the Cat. My whole life flashes before me, the life of a master criminal at the height of his career, at the very peak of his powers.

We land on something hard. Hard like metal, not hard like teeth. I open my eyes a crack and see that we are on the scale that the Enemy uses to weigh cheese. The Cat is there all right, glaring at us nastily, but he makes no move to eat us. He is probably saving us for breakfast.

"So," says the Enemy softly, "these are my clever thieves." He is leaning over us very close, almost touching us with his mustache, peering at us thoughtfully over his spectacles. He looks a little bit like Raymond the Rat when he is thinking.

With this, a faint flicker of hope stirs within me. I remember again that no predicament is so hopeless that it cannot be turned into a victory. All it takes is courage and daring.

Courageously I look the Enemy in the eye. I notice then that his eyes are not really icy steel-gray. They are watery blue with crinkles at the corners.

Suddenly I know there is a chance that the Enemy has a fatal weakness.

I kick Fats. "Stand up," I whisper.

I give Raymond the sharp elbow. "Look ashamed."

My gang seems to catch on. The three of us stand there looking repentant but brave.

"I think it was only that you were hungry," the Enemy says, shaking his head. "You are so very thin." His eyes get more crinkly at the corners.

Now I know we have him. He is soft-hearted.

"Cry," I whisper to Fats.

For once he has no problem obeying. Huge teardrops roll rapidly down his nose and form a puddle on his stomach.

"And what am I to do with you?" the Enemy is asking himself. "Winter comes soon. If I put you outside, what will happen to such small helpless creatures in the snow?"

There is a long silence, during which I look hopeful. The Enemy curls part of his mustache around his finger, just like Raymond does when he is thinking.

Finally, he says, "There is one thing to do. I keep you here in the store with Giovanni and me. There is plenty of cheese to eat, and you will be company for us. I have always liked mice. They remind me of my father's farm in Valenza."

His mustache turns up in a broad smile then, and Fats's tears stop abruptly. We all stand up straight and look honest, clean, brave, kind, thrifty, and cheerful.

Mr. Sammartino gives the Cat a stern look. "You must be nice to our friends, Giovanni," he tells him. "They will live here now."

Giovanni looks resigned.

"The first thing to do," continues Mr. Sammartino, "is make you the nice warm nest." He picks us up, gently this time, and puts us in the pocket of his overcoat.

In the warm darkness we poke each other and shake hands. "Success at last," says Raymond.

"Thanks to me," I add.

CHAPTER FOURTEEN

I GO ON TO BIGGER THINGS

We live the Easy Life. Mr. Sammartino has installed us in an old gray sweater in a cheese carton in the back room and provides an endless supply of cheese from morning to night. Fats devotes most of his time to eating it, and his figure grows rounder every day. Raymond spends hours contentedly reading the New York *Globe* from cover to cover.

Only I am restless. I am tired of being smiled at by Mr. Sammartino. I am tired of staring at the same four walls. I am tired of having all the cheese I can eat. I want action.

One day I say to my gang, "We must eliminate Giovanni."

Fats takes a mammoth bite out of a wedge of Liederkranz. "Why?" he asks lazily.

Raymond looks up from his *Globe*. "He hasn't bothered us, Marvin," he says mildly. "You heard Mr. Sammartino tell him to be nice to us."

"Merciless Marvin," I correct him sharply. "All the same, I don't like the look in his eye. Besides," I go on, giving them the evil stare, "it's time we pulled another job."

They ignore me completely. "I think I'll just take a little nap," mumbles Fats, and he disappears into a sleeve. Raymond turns to the second section of the *Globe*.

After a minute he says, "Here's a story that might interest you, Marvin.

'Thieves Get Away With $50,000 in Madison Avenue Jewel Robbery.' There's a picture and everything."

I peer over Raymond's shoulder at a photograph of the cops looking sadly into an empty safe.

Something about that picture makes up my mind. "Gang," I say, "I have an announcement to make."

As usual, it takes a bit of persuasion to get their attention. Finally, I grab Fats's tail and haul him out of the sleeve. He blinks at me sleepily.

"Ahem," I begin. "Raymond, Fats, good friends, the time has come when I must leave you."

At last I have their undivided attention.

"We have the perfect setup here," I go on. "All the cheese we can eat, an old man with a soft heart, the works. But the Easy Life is not for me. I was meant for bigger things. Jewelry-store jobs, bank jobs—who knows, someday I may even knock over a cheese factory." I pause for dramatic effect. "No, don't try to talk me out of it. My mind is made up."

They protest then, and Fats even cries a little, but I am firm.

That very day I pack up my equipment—a few days' rations of cheese, a coil of stout string, an envelope of pepper. I make a last inspection of the cheese shop, clean up a few crumbs of Kimmel Kase, tweak Giovanni's whiskers in farewell and I am ready to go.

As I slip into my raincoat and felt hat, Raymond says, "Marvin—er, Merciless Marvin—there is something we would like to give you before you leave."

Solemnly he presents me with a gold star from a King's Medal cheese wrapper. "For meritorious leadership above and beyond the call of duty," he proclaims.

Suddenly I begin to feel very fond of my gang. I know I'm going to miss them when I'm on the Outside.

"It was nothing," I tell them. "You couldn't have chosen a worthier leader."

They sing a few choruses of "For He's a Jolly Good Fellow," and Fats does a farewell performance of the glorious cheese dance. Then they walk me to the crack under the door.

"Good-bye forever," cries Fats the Fuse, and Raymond the Rat has a tear in his eye.

"Good-bye, gang," I tell them. "I go to conquer the world."

I slip easily under the door.

Outside I pause and breathe deep. The air is cold but it feels good—wide and empty and full of promises.

I know that I, Merciless Marvin the Magnificent, can handle it.